The Leftover Elf

The
Leftover
Elf

by Mary Stolz

DRAWINGS BY PEGGY BACON

Harper & Row, Publishers
New York and Evanston

THIS IS FOR

Billy

Chapter One

IN THE olden days, in the wild places, there used to be bits of mischief lying about on the ground. These bits of mischief were like small nibbling traps, and they were put about to catch people who came too close to the fairy places. Only an elf could set a mischief trap, and the secret has never been discovered.

This is how they worked . . .

A young man coming home over the fields with a jug of cream under his arm spies some blackberries in a moonlit bramble patch. He thinks to himself, "How glisteny and plump they look. I must have some." Singing a little air, pleased at the prospect of his yellow cream pouring over the blackberries, he approaches the bramble patch. Surely he has no way of knowing that every step brings him closer to an elf house. How could he? People cannot see elves.

The elf, however, hears the footfalls, glances up to see the human form almost upon him. Frowning, he scurries directly into the path of the young man and there sets his trap. The young man steps on it, it snaps, and a stone springs up before him. Since it was not there a moment before, he stumbles over it and sprawls on the ground. His brown jug crashes, the yellow cream streams over the grass, and while the poor young man is rubbing his shins and bewailing his loss, the elf is busily scooping up cream in an acorn shell. Later on, the elf has the cream on a blackberry for dinner, but the poor young man has nothing.

It was not always stones. Sometimes branches swooped down and picked people's hats right off their heads and tossed them toward the sky. Sometimes a tiny cloud would come and rain right on the intruder's head. There was no end to the mischief of a trap.

The elves weren't really bad little creatures, but they had some rather bad habits.

For one thing, they simply could not abide having any human

approach their dwelling places. If a man strayed too close to an elfin house, he was luckless indeed. And as only an animal can see an elf, people were always straying into the traps.

Then, in time, a man was born who grew up and refused to believe in the elves. Everyone else thought he was very foolish and sure to get caught. But as the years went on, they saw that this man could go where he pleased, never having any ill luck at all. He fished in the loneliest streams and hunted through the deepest forests. To be sure, everywhere he went the elf folk frantically set their traps. But because he didn't believe, he trod on the little snares, breaking them all to bits. So people began to think that perhaps the whole thing was an old wives' tale after all. More and more of them put the elf folk out of mind, wandered where they would, and came away freely.

Now, an elf who isn't believed in and doesn't have an elf trap, isn't an elf at all. He just disappears. After a while, only one elf was left.

Their mischief was their undoing.

The leftover elf lived in Ireland. While the other elves were having their mischief traps broken by the feet of people who didn't believe, this elf was going about with his perfectly whole in his pocket, too lazy or too kind to use it.

He wandered about in the deep forest tangles, wondering what had become of everybody. Finally, after about a hundred years, he went to the owl.

Never before had anyone asked the owl anything, although

he was known to be very wise. In the first place, he discouraged conversation by closing his eyes and turning his head when anyone approached him. In the second place, until now nobody had ever wanted to know anything in particular.

Perhaps the long years of not having anyone to talk to had made him lonely, or perhaps he had only been waiting all those years for someone to speak first, but anyway, when the elf came up to him, the owl neither closed his eyes nor turned his head. He didn't say anything, but he looked as though he might answer if spoken to. Taking heart, the elf addressed the owl.

"Oh, Owl," said he, "do you know what has become of everyone?"

"Whooo?" replied the owl. And considering that he had never said a word before, he did very well with this one.

"The other elves," explained the little man. "A few hundred years ago, I noticed there weren't so many of us around. And then one morning I looked all over for the other elves, and there they were ... *gone!*"

"Tooo?" asked the owl.

"I don't know. That's what I'm asking you. Where to?" said the elf, a little vexed.

"Oooo," said the owl.

The elf shook his head. "Just as I thought. The owl knows everything and won't tell anything." And he turned sadly away.

So, for a while, he lived alone, never setting his mischief trap, and not really having much fun. Now and then when he came across a fairy ring in the grass, he would dance in it a little, but dancing alone isn't very gay, and he would soon stop and wander on with a sigh.

One day as he stood beneath a fern to shelter himself from the rain, a tiny frog named Peeper hopped in beside him.

"Hello, Peeper," said the elf with a distant smile.

"Hello, Elf," replied the little frog, "and well met. I have been meaning to talk to you."

"What about?"

"About the other elves," said the frog solemnly.

"Oh, I've already talked about them," the elf said, shaking his head hopelessly.

Peeper blinked. "And whom did you talk to?" he croaked.

The elf heaved a great sigh. "To the owl," he answered.

"What did he say?" asked the curious frog.

"He said, 'who, to, and ooo.' "

"Well, he's not telling all he knows, you can be sure," said the frog, very impressed that the owl had spoken at all.

"Not to me, anyway."

"Now would you like to hear what I think happened?"

The elf didn't look for much help from this quarter, but the frog was a friend, and the elf was always courteous, so he answered, "By all means," thinking to himself that however little the frog knew, it would still be more than he knew himself, so perhaps he could learn something.

[5]

"Well, I think," the frog said hoarsely, "that you people were setting too many of your traps."

"I never set any at all," the elf defended himself. "Except once when a man started to chop down a tree I was living in."

"That's just the point," Peeper told him. "Why should you be left, the only one who didn't set traps? There must be a reason. *That's* the reason."

"What's the reason?" asked the elf.

Peeper looked a little exasperated. "Look here . . . all the others set traps for the slightest reason. They've disappeared. You only set yours once, and that in time of danger. You're still here. Don't you see now?"

The elf thought for a while. "Well," he admitted finally, "there does seem to be a connection." Then he lapsed into thought again.

"But that's not all," said Peeper. "I only happen to know what I'm going to tell you now because I accidentally got carried off with some turf for a fire in the village." He shuddered, recalling the experience.

"What a *terrible* thing," sympathized the elf.

"Terrible," repeated the frog. "However, I managed to wriggle through the peat, and then I waited by the cottage door for someone to open it. I'm so small that no one ever noticed me, and the first time the door opened, I hopped out. But what I started to tell you," he went on, after the elf had congratulated him heartily on this escape, "was what I heard in the cottage.

[7]

"While I was waiting by the door, I listened to the people talking, and they were saying things about elves. What I heard will really shock you, but I think you should know." He paused, as though figuring how best to put the dreadful news. The elf waited nervously, but said nothing. Finally the frog went on. "It seems," he said carefully, "that the people don't—believe in elves any more."

Then the elf's eyes grew wide with horror, but try as he would, he could not say a word.

"Now, I gathered from the bits I heard," the frog continued, picking up a leaf to fan the elf in case he grew faint, "that the people got tired of being caught in mischief traps. So when they found out that by not believing either in the elves or their traps, they didn't get caught . . . well, they simply all stopped be-lieving."

"Oh my, oh my, oh my," groaned the unhappy elf, "whatever is to become of me? However have I lasted this long? For sure I'm going to dissolve. Because never an elf can live if no one believes in him." He groaned again, feeling himself to see if he'd already started to melt away.

"Now pull yourself together," said Peeper, a little sternly. "You're still here, so there must be a reason. All we have to do is figure out what it is. And, for a fact," he added, "I seem to be doing all the figuring."

"I'm sorry, Peeper," replied the elf dismally. "I'll try to help. But it isn't you that's going to melt away . . ."

"You're not going to melt away. All the others disappeared ages ago, because of their mischief. You didn't bother much with mischief, so that must be part of the reason you're still here. But now what can the other part be?" So much thinking having made him a little hot-headed, Peeper began to fan himself with the leaf.

So they sat beneath the fern, thinking as hard as they could. The rain stopped, but they didn't notice. Green twilight moved up behind them, passed over, dragging the night with it, but they didn't notice. Dawn inched over the mountain and gradually spread over the sky like rosy ink on a dark blotter. Still they didn't notice.

Then when the first bird call sounded briefly in the morning air, the frog spoke.

"Elf," he announced, "I know now."

"What?" asked the elf, half anxiously, half fearfully.

"Somewhere there is somebody who still believes in you," the frog said in a sure tone.

"Really? Are you sure?" asked the elf, taking heart.

"Positive. There can be no other answer."

The elf nodded. "I can't imagine who it could be," he said.

"Well, of course not," croaked Peeper.

"How can I find out?" the elf went on, half to himself.

The frog stared in bewilderment. "Find out?" he stammered. "You can't possibly find out. Why should you want to find out?

You couldn't. And even if you did, where would you be then? What *are* you thinking of?"

"Well," the elf said hesitantly, "if there really is someone who believes in me, I'd like to see him. Her, maybe."

"Why?"

"I just would. Maybe thank him, or something," murmured the elf feebly.

The frog stared at the elf, his heavy-lidded eyes filled with amazement. "Elf," he said slowly, "I'm sorry I ever told you about this. I can see it is going to lead to nothing but trouble. For years, hundreds and thousands of years, you elves lived happily in the wild places. You never left them. You never went searching for people who believed in you, to thank them or do anything else about them. They did, and because they did, you lived. It was enough. It is enough now."

"But perhaps whoever it is will stop," the elf cried.

"And what could you do about that? People can't see you, can't hear you. You couldn't thank them at all. Please, Elf, stay here where you belong." Peeper seemed so distressed that the elf hesitated.

"But Peeper—." The elf stopped. He could see there was no way of explaining how he, as the last elf, must discover the Believer and try in some way to revive the old beliefs, so maybe the elves would come back. "Only this time," he thought to himself, "they should try not to be so handy with the traps." He became lost in a dream in which fairies once again capered through the hills of Ireland. It all became so real to him that a smile of pleasure lit up his tiny face.

The frog, noting the smile, despaired of making his point. So he hopped away, and his hopping was heavy with sorrow. Hop, thud. Hop, thud. Hop, thud. Off he went, into the ferny places, feeling quite sad, and wondering at the same time whether he would find a bug or two, because he hadn't had anything to eat for quite a while. A stomach does have a way of getting in front of a sorrow.

The elf, left by himself beneath the fern, thought nothing of food. He thought only of his plan to find the Believer. He would take a trip, he decided, and keep going until he found the Believer.

This was a very encouraging idea, and the elf certainly felt better than he had in a long time.

Chapter Two

IN THE fairy world, thoughts have time to gather meaning, since nothing is ever in a hurry to happen, or to stop happening. So, for several years, the elf passed his time pleasantly enough, letting the idea of a Trip to Find the Believer rock about in his head, developing slowly.

And the frog, who had been so sad, gradually forgot the night that he and the elf had sat under the fern finding an answer.

He had forgotten it so completely that when a morning came on which he searched high and low for his friend the elf, without result, he became quite frantic. Over the hills and through the forests he hopped, searching. And since the hop of a tiny frog is tiny too, it took him many months to cover all the ground he knew. His search began in the spring. In the autumn, he sadly concluded that the last believer had abandoned his belief, and that the little elf had dissolved.

With a heavy heart, he started back to the forest glen where he and the elf had spent so many happy days.

But, you see, he was wrong, so it was a pity the elf had not been able to write him a little note. This is what had happened . . .

Early on a spring morning, when the world seemed to be fairly snapping with freshness, the elf awoke from his sleep with a plan all settled in his head. It hadn't been there the night before when he curled up beneath his blanket, which was softer than silk and had been spun for him by a spider of his acquaintance. So the plan must have come along sometime during the night, and had no doubt crept in with one of his dreams.

This plan started whispering as soon as the elf awoke. "Elf," it whispered, "the Trip to Find the Believer should start today."

"Should it now?" answered the elf, but not out loud, since the plan could hear him perfectly well when he just thought, being up there in his head.

"Best possible day for it," replied the plan cozily.

And the more the elf considered the chirpiness and charm of the bright spring morning, the more he knew that this was entirely so.

Accordingly, he took from his pocket an object of great value. It was a pocket handkerchief, once the possession of a man in the village, which had, a long time ago and by great good fortune, blown off a hedge of sunning wash right into the hand of the elf, who had happened to be passing. It was a handkerchief of pure Irish linen, and considered a prize by all beholders. This handkerchief he now spread out carefully on the moss, placing in it the things he felt necessary for his trip.

First, his cobweb blanket, folded with care. Then a few nuts. Then a pine needle and some corn silk, in case he needed to do some mending. Finally he placed his mischief trap on top of the other things, but then took it out and put it back in his pocket. He knotted the four corners of the handkerchief, tied it to the end of a twig, swung the bundle over his shoulder and started off.

No particular way. Just off.

He looked around for Peeper as he went, but as luck would have it, he met neither his friend the frog, nor anyone of their mutual acquaintance. So that was how it turned out that he neither told Peeper good-bye, nor left him any message of comfort and farewell.

The elf bounded along, leaving the forest far behind. Over the fields of clover and shamrock he went, his pocket-handkerchief bundle bobbing gaily, his little scarlet hat twinkling like a flower on the move.

And all around him the Spring chortled.

The pied plumage of a magpie flickered from a juniper clump across his path. A bright-winged butterfly fanned slowly by, rising and descending in great slow arcs. A swallow shot past in an ecstasy of flight.

"My," thought the little elf, "there certainly are pretty things in the air."

He sprang to the top of a rock, and stood with his legs apart, cockily surveying the sky, where fat little clouds tumbled in a blue field.

A sigh of pure contentment escaped him, and the plan, which had been relaxing comfortably, almost got carried out with it. "Here now!" protested the plan, "you almost blew me away."

"Oh, my goodness, I'd forgotten all about you," the elf remarked in surprise.

"Well, we'll never get anything done that way, you know. If I fell out and got lost some place, you'd have to go back to the forest. And I don't know if another plan would ever find you at all. So be a little more careful," the plan grumbled, "or you never will find the Believer."

"Oh, I will, to be sure," said the elf, in some alarm. "We'll go along immediately."

Leaping down from the rock, the elf set firmly off in any direction at all, which eventually led him to a road, along the side of which ran a low stone wall. Along the top of this wall the elf went skipping, remembering not to let his light heart sigh, or at least not too hard, since without his plan he would surely never figure out how to find the Believer.

"Although," he thought to himself, "so far it hasn't given me much in the way of directions."

"I heard that," the plan retorted vigorously. "There's no point to giving directions till we get to a town. Or until we see some people."

They went on in silence for a while. Then the elf said, "Look here, do you have to listen to everything I think?"

"I can't help it. I'm up here where all the thinking is. Try being quieter."

"That's silly. You can't think quieter."

"How about not thinking at all?"

"That's impossible," protested the elf.

"Certainly is not. I've been in heads where there wasn't a thought from morning till night. Of course," the plan added, "those were people's heads. You're my first elf."

"What's a people head like?"

"Bigger," answered the plan. "Cluttered. But some of them aren't bad."

"Maybe you've been around the Believer," the elf said eagerly, subsiding when the plan replied, "No, I'm sorry. And I don't know any plans that have. But don't you worry, we'll find him."

Worry was the farthest thing from the elf's thoughts. Who indeed could worry on such a day? The gentlest of breezes winged idly along, flirting through the spinneys at the wall's edge, tugging carelessly at the elf's feathered hat, dandling some meadow-sweet because it smelled so nice.

A stream leaped through the fields, singing the clear cool song that all streams know. At one point it dove under the road, to reappear at the other side, chanting over round smooth rocks, plunging into a tiny cataract, streaking off behind a clump of birches.

Oh, much too fine a day to worry on.

The elf went along, following the road itself after the wall dwindled to just a few stones clasped by ivy fingers. Dusted with warm brown earth the road lay, sprawling along without ambition.

"I couldn't have picked a better day," the elf congratulated himself.

"*Who* couldn't have picked a better day?" inquired the plan.

"Well, you couldn't," conceded the elf in high humor. "By the way, can you see all right?"

"Perfectly. I'm looking through your eyes, you know."

"Are you now?" said the elf in amazement. "What a funny way to look at things."

"Oh, I always try to see things through other's eyes. That's one of the nicest things about being a plan. It's so sharing."

The elf considered this for a while, then inquired, "How about when you aren't in someone's head, what do you do then?"

"Go around looking for someone who seems to need a plan. Then I slip into his head, find out what's needed, and turn into that sort of plan."

"I didn't know you could change around that way," said the elf, more and more surprised.

"Didn't know—. For heaven's sake, if we plans couldn't change ourselves, there wouldn't be any order in the world at all. There aren't enough of us to go around as it is. That's why there's so much confusion. How many times do you suppose a plan for a Trip to Find the Believer is needed?"

"Hasn't anyone else ever looked for a Believer?" asked the elf shyly.

"Oh, yes," said the plan, a little sorry for being so abrupt. "But more often for a belief."

"Do they find one?"

"Sometimes."

By this time they had reached a little rise in the road, and on the other side, quite far back from the road, they saw a small farm. As they watched, a cow came swaying out of the barn, and behind her a girl, carrying a bucket of frothing milk.

Suddenly the elf began to run.

"Wisha, what's all the hurry for?" protested the plan, who was being flung about rather badly.

"Maybe . . ." panted the elf, "maybe that girl . . . the Believer, you know . . ."

"Slow down!"

The elf did, but not very much.

"You don't think," continued the plan, having managed to get upright again, "that you're going to find the Believer so quickly, do you?"

"And why not?" asked the elf, walking very fast.

"I never heard tell of anyone at all finding what he was after so quickly. Of course, you may be different," he said. "Only I don't think so."

By now they had arrived at the gate to the little farm. Hopping over the pickets, the tiny fellow landed on a grain of corn, just as a burly red hen reached for it.

"Ow!" shrieked the elf, as a sharp yellow beak jabbed his soft shoe.

"Get off my corn!" snapped the hen.

Pouting, the elf moved aside. "I didn't mean to step on your

[19]

corn, Biddy," he said, eying the hen mischievously, because, as is well known, hens do not care to be addressed as Biddy, preferring the more formal Madame Cluck.

Glaring, the hen advanced. "Address your biggers respectfully, you red-headed grasshopper," she gritted fiercely.

The elf slapped his knees and laughed. "I'm not a grasshopper. I'm an elf."

"Never heard of you," muttered the hen.

The elf was a little dashed by this, but the spell of the day was on him, so he remarked pleasantly enough, "This is a very pretty farm."

The hen regarded him blankly, then turned an equally blank eye on the little farmyard, with its whitewashed house and barn, its brilliant disorder of flowers.

"Is it?" she said. "I never noticed."

The elf gaped. "You mean you live here and never see how fine it is?"

"I have no time for idleness," replied the hen. "What with eggs to be laid, and eating when she calls us, to say nothing of picking up all these bits of corn and grain that are scattered about so carelessly, I never have time to look at anything but the ground." And she went on pick, pick, picking very virtuously.

"Who's she?" asked the elf, not to be turned aside by bad manners.

"Who's who?"

"She. You said when she calls us. I mean you, calls you." The elf sauntered after the red chicken, whose picking was taking her away from the fence toward the barn.

"Oh," replied the hen, halting for a moment. "She's the one who just went by with the bucket of milk. Now that she's attended to the pigs and the horse and the cow, she'll get around to feeding us chickens, who are certainly the hardest workers on the farm, *and* the most important, but . . ."

"Are you always this disagreeable?" interrupted the elf curiously.

The hen ruffled all her feathers with rage, stalked away without answering. Shaking his head, the elf watched her haughty retreat, then ran in pursuit. "Look now, I'm sorry, Bid—I mean, Madame Cluck. I didn't mean to be rude," he said coaxingly. "Talk to me some more, please." Although why he wished to talk with such an unobliging chicken puzzled the plan, who had been listening. The hen accepted his apology rather sulkily, and they continued their conversation. The plan found that so dull that he curled up and went to sleep.

Presently a great stir of excitement ran through the company of hens. The elf looked about eagerly to discover the cause, and saw a resplendent figure stalk nobly through the barn door. With lofty carriage, flashing eye, the beautiful one proceeded through the throng of hens, while the elf gazed entranced.

"Now there," he remarked, "is a broth of a hen."

Several chickens turned to stare at him in horror, and one whispered loudly, "You fool! That is . . . the ROOSTER!"

At the sound of his title, the great one turned his head and allowed his eyes to rest approvingly upon the speaker. He disregarded the elf altogether, which was just as well, and resumed his promenade.

His tail flared so elegantly. His feathers gleamed so vividly. His hens adored so openly. Truly, it was very impressive. Even when he flapped rather heavily trying to attain the fence, it mattered not. Having achieved a balance, the rooster lifted his head and rendered such a mighty solo that the elf almost decided to settle down among the chickens so as to remain always in the company of this master. Then another call mingled with, and overreached, the song of Chanticleer.

"Chick, chick, chickchickchick," it wheedled. The girl appeared, with a large basin under her arm. "Chickchickchick, chick, chick," she called, low and enticing, as she showered grain from the basin.

With heads straining forward, eyes bugging out, yellow claws digging in the ground, the chickens tore past the astonished elf, who was whirled dizzily about as hen after cackling hen rushed past him toward the feast.

Turning to comfort the rooster, thus vulgarly deserted, the elf was shocked to see, in a beating of wings and a flash of color, the proud one hurl himself into the fray.

"Just a chicken, after all," realized the elf.

In disillusion, he chose to leave the farm. Before going, he vaulted to the fence post, and, lifting his head, shrilled a mocking imitation of the proud cock's call, to which no one listened.

Then, leaping down, he continued his journey.

Chapter Three

ONE MORNING, well into the summer, the elf, who was having such a good time wandering about that he had almost forgotten his purpose, was sunning himself on a large flat rock and munching on the last of his store of nuts. He heard a creaking and a sound of voices coming from beyond a bend in the road. Not the same road, but one that looked very much the same, as roads do.

Full of curiosity, the little fellow waited as the sounds grew louder and nearer. He spied a pair of long grey ears coming round the bend. Which ears were followed by a small grey donkey. Hitched to the small grey donkey was a little creaking cart. Beside the cart walked two men.

"Now, Francis," the younger one was saying earnestly, "don't you be wondering where it went, because it's a sure thing you won't be seeing it agin, not in this world you won't." Though the old man seemed distracted with grief, the younger went on lightly, "It's the fortunes of the world."

"Devil take you with your fortunes of the world, Harry," the old one said angrily. "This was my own private particular fortune." He shook his head mournfully.

"Tell me again how you got it," said Harry soothingly. "Maybe that will take your mind off it."

"Take my mind off it!" bellowed the other. "How will that take my mind off it? Nothing will. I tell you, Harry McDonough, my entire life is destroyed." He left off talking altogether.

The little donkey jerked an ear up, then let it flap loosely down again. The two men plodded on in silence. In the cart a great assortment of pots and pans jostled their dented sides together.

"Tinkers, that's what they are," decided the elf, and he waited on his rock, very curious. But the two men didn't seem disposed for conversation. So the elf did a reasonable thing. He perched atop one of the pots in the cart and jogged along with the small company, awaiting developments.

[26]

He was beginning to think that they would all go on in silence through whatever was left of time, when Francis began to mutter. "I tell you," he said, more to himself than to Harry McDonough, "it's a hard cruel world, when an old man loses the only dear little gold piece he ever had in his whole long life. His whole long life," he repeated in a low keening voice. "One little gold piece, and some miserable, scurvy, scoundrel of a thief steals it."

"Hold on now, Francis. I'm the only one that's been with you, so you're after calling me a thief, and that I won't have," said Harry.

"Ahh, forgive me, Harry, I don't know what I'm saying at all." Francis halted with sudden decision. "Harry," he announced firmly, "I'm going back over the road and search again."

Harry took a deep breath before he spoke. "*Francis* . . . We've been looking over the road. And over the fields, and over the ditches, and over the whole blathering county. We've looked places we've never been to begin with, and we're wasting our time. Now I'm going on to Kilcoole and try to find a job of tinkering. Are you coming with me, or are you not?"

Perplexed and miserable, Francis squinted at his companion, saying nothing.

The little grey donkey turned his head, pawed at the dust, shook his harness, then stood in quiet waiting. The elf hopped from pot to pan, rattling them a bit, but no one noticed. The yellow sun beat down on the two men, who stood staring at each other in utter quandary.

"Francis," Harry pleaded, "where was it when you lost it?"

"Where was it? In my hand, of course. Where else would it be?"

"Well, have you looked in your hand?"

Cautiously, Francis turned his eyes down to his clenched fist, and slowly opened it. There, prettily gleaming, was a round gold piece.

For a moment there was silence. Then Harry clacked his tongue at the donkey. The four little hoofs began to clop, and the pots and pans resumed their clattering.

Francis and Harry trudged along, unspeaking, on their way to Kilcoole. After a long time, Francis spoke. "Harry?"

Silence from Harry.

"Harry, my boy."

A sidelong glance from Harry.

"Odd thing, that." Francis gazed appealingly at his friend.

His friend nodded and stared at the road.

"I'll make it up to you, Harry. Half this piece is yours, from this moment forward. When we get to Kilcoole, we'll make ourselves easy, like a pair of princes. We'll put up at the Inn, and the pots and pans can await our pleasure."

Old Francis stepped briskly along, so that the little donkey broke into a trot, and Harry brightened, lengthening the stride of his long legs. Down the long road that wrapped around the mountain and tapered to the sea they went, and so toward Kilcoole, which is a nice town on the east coast of Ireland, where tinkers, even tinkers who do not intend to tinker, can always find a welcome.

The elf had been thinking very loud and hard for quite some time, trying to awaken the plan, who seemed to be getting hazier and lazier as the summer went on. Which is the way with some plans, who simply cannot see things through.

But finally the elf managed to stir it into wakefulness long enough to inquire whether they should continue with the tinkers.

"What tinkers?" asked the plan grumpily.

"Oh, my goodness," exclaimed the elf, "haven't you been paying any attention?"

"Sort of," came the drowsy reply. "Are these the same two who were arguing about the gold piece?"

"They are. And they're still talking about it. Not arguing any more, though."

"Well," said the plan, after considering for a while and nearly falling asleep again, "I think we might as well go into Kilcoole with them, and then look around the town."

So the elf remained swinging on a pot handle while the cart descended creakily to the town by the coast. Through the trees he could see the wide waters of the ocean sloping toward the shore, and he could hear the hoarse breakers far below.

Down and down wound the road, till at last it edged off the mountain and ran levelly along to meet the cobbled streets of Kilcoole.

Twilight had come rapidly, and in the cottages the oil lamps were lit. The tinkers stopped their cart before an inn. Because there was no breeze, the sign above the door hung motionless. Its cheerful legend, *Hand and Bottle*, coupled with the sound of jovial voices within, was very tempting to two men with a grand gold piece between them.

With one accord, they directed the donkey's steps toward the stable. There the elf left them.

Chapter Four

THROUGH THE gloaming he hopped and skipped, till he came to a small thatched cottage, round which the spired hollyhocks were just beginning to close. Bars of lamplight poled through the small windows, and when the elf hopped to the open upper half of the door, he saw some people sitting around a table, eating their evening meal.

They were having potatoes, of course, and meat that sent up a fragrant steam. A big pudding quivered in the middle of the table, waiting to be dessert.

The elf clambered into the house and ran up one of the chairs to the table top, thinking that to be invisible to people was very handy when hungry. He stole a little bit of food from each plate, munching comfortably as he moved between them. When he got to the pudding, he hesitated. Taking food which the people were already eating had been quite easy, since no one noticed the bits that disappeared. But to attack the smooth expanse of untouched pudding was riskier, and since the dish was so high, there was always the danger of falling in, which would be messy and noticeable.

So he chose to wait until everyone was served, hoping, in the meantime, to hear some conversation.

But there wasn't any.

Never had the elf been to a dinner (uninvited, to be sure) like this. There were six people at the table, and they all stared at their plates, never moving their eyes unless toward another dish for direction in getting more food. No friendly banter, no discussions, no exchange of any views at this dull table.

It is not a pleasant way to eat, and the elf became so annoyed that he decided to skip the dessert course altogether. So to the door and out into the garden, which by now was quite dark.

He found himself standing beneath a trumpet vine, with red blossoms tightened in sleep, while all around him the gentle darkness kept its secrets. The night sounds rose from the grass, as the day sounds fall from the air.

As he stood listening, a powerful softness engulfed the elf and flung him to the ground. The grey hunter in the night held him beneath her paw. The Cat.

The paw edged carefully over, so that the elf could thrust his head, from which the little hat had tumbled, out through fur and claws. A pink nose quivered close to him, sniffing. A pair of sand-gold eyes examined him minutely. Finally the paw turned back slowly, and the elf was able to crawl out and retrieve his hat.

While he was giving a slight fillip to his hairdo before replacing his cap, the cat eyed him thoughtfully. "What in the world are you?" she questioned, turning her head from one side to the other.

"I'm an elf," said the little fellow with dignity.

The cat, whose own family line is very long, remembered some ancient tales concerning elves, and was quite pleased to be actually seeing one. She said as much.

"That's nice," commented the elf a little sourly. "Next time try to see me before you pounce."

"I feel dreadful about that," apologized the cat. "But I'm out for an evening's hunt. I thought you were something tasty, that's all. I hope you'll forgive me." She sounded very upset, and the elf, never one to refuse a graceful apology, assured her of his pardon. The cat invited him to spend some time with her in the barn, where she and her kittens lived.

"Tell me," the elf asked drowsily as they lay in the warm straw, "don't those people in the house ever talk?"

"Oh, they have nothing to say to each other."

"Why not? They live together. How can people live together and not talk?"

"They talk, I suppose. Things like, 'Is there any left?' or, 'If you don't hurry, I'm not going to wait,' but never just fooling around with words. And never about anything that matters."

"How awful," said the elf.

"There are really a great many people like that. Didn't you know?"

"I certainly didn't. And I'm sorry I found out."

"Why?"

"Because the more people there are of that sort, the less chance I'll have of finding my Believer. He'd certainly never be anyone who was too flattened out to talk."

The cat looked very interested, so the elf had to explain all about it. When he was finished, she remarked that she had wondered why no one talked much about the elf people, and was very hopeful that he would have good fortune in his search.

Then they talked about other things for a while, and eventually fell asleep, the cat stretched out calmly beside her kittens, the elf wrapped up in his beautiful frail blanket.

He stayed with the cat family for quite a while, because he found the cat and the flickering, tail-and-butterfly chasing kittens so charming.

And then, the cat was so well informed.

"You know," she remarked one day as they strolled through

an adjoining field, "I'm very fond of poetry. In fact, sometimes I make up verses." She looked at the ground demurely.

"I'd like to hear some," was the elf's very proper reply.

The cat sat down and closed her eyes for a moment in concentration. "This is one of my favorites. I call it *The Huntscat of the Sky.*

> *"The moon is so shy.*
> *She's caught in the jaws*
> *Of the midnight sky.*
> *So I dart my paws*
> *In the teethy stars*
> *To flick her through.*
> *I'll make no scars,*
> *That would never do.*
> *Sheathe my claws*
> *As I scoop at the moon,*
> *If I get my paws*
> *On her, I will soon*
> *Set her free of the midnight sky.*
> *I wouldn't eat her . . . no, not I."*

There was silence.

Then the elf said, "It's pretty." When the cat made no reply, he went on slowly. "It makes me a little—a little nervous." He added, "I don't suppose it makes you nervous?"

"No," said the cat, "it doesn't. But then, I know what I had in mind, and you don't. That would account for it."

"Mmm," said the elf. "But it is pretty."

They talked of other things.

"I like music," said the elf on another morning, when they sat on a rock to get the sun.

"Oh, I do too," his hostess agreed. "I like nothing so much as a group of Toms singing in the night. It's the only true music, you know," she added firmly, and leaped down from the rock, bowled over a passing kitten, pinned it to the ground, and commenced washing it vigorously.

The elf, who had heard tomcats singing in the night and did not think it was music at all, was going to say that he had meant bird songs. He remembered how the birds had sung in the early morning back in his wild place, and that was what he called music. But it wasn't a subject he felt would be welcome to the cat, who certainly had opinions about birds, but of rather a different sort.

He had begun to get rather lonely for his home, and now he toyed with the idea of turning back. It was well into the summer, and he didn't seem to be any closer to his Believer than he'd been that night under the fern. Thinking of the night under the fern made him miss his friend the frog so much that he jumped up, with full intention of bidding the cat good-bye and setting back.

"No, no, no. None of that!" said a voice close by.

The elf peered about in bewilderment. "Did you say something?" he inquired of the cat, who had a mouthful of fur and only answered, "Hmmm?"

"Now don't say you've forgotten all about me?" said the same voice in a wounded tone.

"Oh, my goodness," gulped the elf. "Where have you been all this time?"

"Up here, patiently waiting," answered the plan. "I have been waiting for you to finish this holiday in the hayloft and get on with what we set out to do. You've been loafing around here with Mistress Puss for weeks. I'll admit we've learned a lot, but we didn't start out for an education, you know."

The elf admitted that.

"Well, say good-bye, and let's get on with this junket."

With promises of a future meeting, the elf set off down the road. Once he looked back, to see the big cat again on the rock. In the blue rock shadow, the kittens tumbled each other.

Chapter Five

ONE EVENING found the elf down by the wharves. He perched on a sea wall and watched the tug-boats on the water. They looked warm and friendly in the dark, with lights in their cabins and men sitting on the decks placidly smoking their pipes.

Sometimes, when they came close enough, the elf could hear their voices. All along the shore the yellow lights streamed out into the night and over the bay, rising and sinking with the waves.

A sea gull skimmed low over the water, banked against the air and sailed sideways to a perch on the sea wall, where he stood teetering for a moment, wings outstretched. Then he folded them and waddled toward the elf.

"Awwk," he screeched in greeting.

"Awk to you, sir," said the little man, always happy to have a conversation.

"And how do you find yourself?" inquired the gull cordially.

" 'Tisn't myself that wants finding. It's someone else."

"If you've found yourself, that's the most important part. Let the others go." The gull nodded his head sagely. "That's the trouble with you human beings. You're always prying around with other people, instead of attending to yourselves."

"I'm not a human being. I'm . . . "

"You aren't?" interrupted the sea gull with surprise. "You look just like one. What there is of you," he added doubtfully.

"I'm an elf."

"An elf? Can't say I've heard of you, but pleased to make your acquaintance."

"So am I. To meet you."

The elf studied the gull closely, with more interest than manners, but the bird didn't seem to mind. He really appeared a bit flattered. The elf thought he had seldom seen an uglier face, with its little black snapping eyes close to the hooked bill. But the sea gull had sleek smoky feathers, and a friendly note in his harsh voice. Anyway, since his experience with the rooster, the elf did not place his affection too quickly in the lap of beauty.

"Have you ever been out to sea?" he asked the gull. "Far out, I mean?"

"Lots of times. I follow the ships for miles."

"Did you ever see a whale?" asked the elf, who had heard about whales from the cat. She had a sea-going cousin.

"Big thing, a whale." The gull nodded his head. "Yes, I've seen them. I even sat on a while for a whale once. I mean a whale for a while."

The elf giggled, which was apparently what the sea gull wanted, because he preened his feathers happily and beamed upon the elf.

"The ships look so wonderful. I'd like to sail on one some-time," the elf remarked dreamily.

"Really shouldn't call it sailing any more. Call it steaming, or chugging, or what-have-you. No sails nowadays, not to speak of. All done with turbines. Not very romantic."

"But safer, I should think."

"They still sink. Which is all right for the ship, mind you.

Only proper end for a ship. But the people on them do a lot of fussing. Awwk."

This seemed reasonable, but the elf said nothing, since he had never learned to disagree with people who seemed sure of themselves.

They sat in a comfortable silence, the elf watching the waterfront lights riding on the waves, the sea gull smoothing his feathers. And all around them the boisterous human voices resounded. The elf had never seen quite so many people all in one place before. They sauntered along on the wet cobblestones, singing, laughing, shouting, bullying. Whatever they did, they did it louder than any other people the elf had ever heard.

"What noisy people," he said.

The gull picked up his head. "Well," he said, "you have to remember that you're among sailors now. When you're down on the wharves, you aren't exactly hobnobbing with society. For my taste," he went on, "you won't find a better lot of humans. But of course you may feel differently about it."

"Oh, they seem very nice to me," protested the elf. "It's just that I'm used to quieter places."

"It's quiet enough out at sea. I suppose that's one of the reasons they make so much noise on shore. People are different from the rest of us. Take me," said the gull. "I'm a sea gull. Fly about, catch a fish now and then, settle on the water, fly up from the water. Spend my life that way. Now, as far as I know, most animals and birds are perfectly content to find one day just like another day, all their lives. They don't want changes. But people want them all the time. If they have a long rest, they have to work for a change. If they work hard, they have to rest for a change. They're always having to do something for a change. Which is probably," he concluded, "the reason these sailors make so much racket. A change from the quiet of the sea."

All this time the fog had been sidling in. First little twinings that gradually joined to form a great mantle which closed over the entire water front.

With a hoarse "awwk," the sea gull flew off into the vaporous air. Left alone, the elf sat motionless, waiting. He was sure the sea gull would come back, because there had been no farewells. In a little while he saw the powerful wings come beating slowly toward him through the fog.

Gripped in that ferocious-looking beak, the elf could see a little fish with glistening silver scales. The gull dropped to the water just below, and rode the swell of the waves. As he glanced up to the elf, his fish disappeared into the water with a flashing wriggle.

For a second, the sea gull's eyes flared with anger. Then he laughed. "Serves me right," he said. "That's the first time I ever lost a fish that was right in my mouth. Very stupid of me. Was going to invite you to have some, and when I opened my mouth our snack got away. I'll go get another directly, because I'm sure you must be hungry."

"I guess I am, but really, don't get another fish for me. You're very kind, but I'm afraid I don't like raw fish."

"You don't?" The sea gull mused over the possibilities. "What do you eat? Seaweed?"

The elf had to admit that he didn't think he ate seaweed either. "I just eat around," he explained. "I like all the things people do, but in the woods I eat best. Berries, mushrooms, you know."

The sea gull didn't, but he nodded. "Well," he said, after he'd wondered what a mushroom was like, and decided he didn't care, since chances were he'd never eat one, "I've got to get back to my fishing. Do you think you'll be around long?"

"I guess I'll go find something to eat, too, so perhaps I won't be seeing you again," the elf said regretfully. "I never do seem to get back anywhere."

"That's all right," the gull assured him. "You keep going ahead, which is a good thing. I'm glad to have met you, and you'll be in my thoughts from time to time."

The elf smiled warmly. He liked the sea gull. Then, with a parting "Awwk," the gull disappeared into the fog.

Now the human voices were fewer, and muffled by the fog. The elf could hear the water slapping at the sea wall, but all he could see were the globed street lights suspended mistily in air. It was beginning to rain.

"Well," he thought pointedly, to prod the plan into response, "what do we do now?"

The plan, who was feeling a bit agley, replied confusedly, "I'm not sure. Perhaps you should go home after all. Or, no . . . that wouldn't do. Possibly you should try . . . Look, I really don't know what to do. We don't seem to be getting anywhere at all, do we?"

The elf was quite irritated and didn't try to conceal it. "I've certainly done my part," he said, a bit unfairly. "I've wandered all over the country, while you've done nothing but sleep or preach at me."

"Oh, now," the plan protested, really hurt. "It hasn't been as bad as all that. After all, we did get to see a lot, and you've met some interesting people. You've had a nice summer, haven't you?"

"Yes," admitted the little fellow. "But I could have had a nice summer at home. How am I ever going to get people to believe in elves if I can't even find the one who believes in me?"

The plan sighed. "Elf," he said, "let's try once more, and then if we fail, I shall have to admit that I'm a useless plan. I will leave you, and perhaps you'll find a better plan than I have been." He sobbed once, then made a brave effort to rally.

The elf was overcome with remorse. After all, he *had* had a fine summer, and the plan had been a good companion. "I have been an ungrateful creature. Will you forgive me?" he begged of the tearful plan, who hiccoughed and accepted.

By now very hungry, the elf set off in search of food. Along the shrouded streets he went, looking for an open door, an open window. But it seemed that every house had sealed itself against the bleak night. All he saw were thin chinks of light at barred doors. And more than total darkness, these slivers of light seemed to say, "Closed, closed, we're all closed."

Buffeted softly by the slipping silver paws of the rain, the elf huddled miserably against one of these stern doors. And so found himself in a warm, bright, exquisitely fragrant kitchen. Because just as he leaned against it, someone inside opened the door, spilling out a square of yellow light, and toppling in the little lonely elf.

Scrambling to get out of feet's way, the elf sped happily into a corner, there to shiver with delight at the warmth, to gaze with ecstasy around the busy kitchen.

So many odors vied with each other in the kitchen that the air was a scented battleground. From little hot jars of newly bottled jelly, a grape spiciness rose to tilt with the lusty smell of roasting meat. Above them a redolence of dark plum cake fenced merrily with a legion of odors marching up from the loaves of bread. Within the oven a nutty breakfast ring planned its strategy, while a bland custard haughtily refused to join the fight.

Moving amidst the crocks, the pipkins, the iron roasting pans, was a stout comfortable woman with a round face that had an appley glow to it. She had made all these things that were sending their hot odors into battle. She had the look that all good cooks have . . . proud and pleased.

It was a great big kitchen, and everything in it was big. The round table, set for dinner, the black stove, the fireplace and the blaze within. Everything in it was clean. The chipped and gleaming china, the odd assortment of sparkling glasses, the mended muslin curtains. Over the stove a row of copper pots reflected the fire.

In a rocking chair, close to the fire, sat an old man. He rocked sedately back and forth, watching the mealtime preparations. "Daisy," he addressed the stout woman, "Daisy, my girl, when will we eat? I'm that hungry I feel like a squeezed accordion."

"In a moment, Dad," came the reply, and the old man sighed happily. So did the elf.

The door to the kitchen was flung open. In marched two strong men, a young woman, and three children who shone from a recent soaping. This entire company, together with the old man and Daisy, assembled round the big table. The elf thought confidently to himself that here was one family that wouldn't sit silent through a meal.

He was right. As he moved about the table, following his custom of eating just a little from each plate, he wondered how in the world they ever heard each other. Everybody seemed to be talking at once.

As they laughed and shouted and answered and sent the food around the table, the elf sorted them out, because he liked to keep things clear.

The children were Peggy, Tommy and Emmett. Emmett was the smallest. The young woman and man were their parents, the older man and Daisy their grandparents. And the old man was their great-grandfather. "Which," said the elf to himself, "is certainly an honorable estate."

Dinner took a long time. But when it was finished, and the cleaning up done, the family began to disappear upstairs, till only Daisy and the old man were left.

Daisy yawned widely. "Dad," she asked, "are you going to bed like a proper person, or are you going to sit up and get tired?"

"I believe I'll sit here a bit, my girl, and remember a few old things. But not get tired."

"Well, I'm tired now," said Daisy. She bent over to put a kiss on the ruddy wrinkled brow. "See you in the morning."

"In the mornin', Daisy."

The kitchen, emptied of the family, seemed even bigger than before, but the bright warmth lingered. Even a few of the odors were left. Too faint to fight any more, they were idling around in the air, waiting to dissolve.

By the chimney, Granddad nodded gently. His pipe dangled in his fingers, slipped a little, dangled some more, then dropped quietly to the floor. In the hearth, the logs crackled in a muted way, as though the fire, too, were drowsy. Nodding, nodding, the old man's head fell forward.

Now the silence was all around.

For a while, the elf sat forlornly, wondering what to do. The plan said no word, no matter how hard the elf thought to it. He sighed. He wandered aimlessly about the kitchen. He sighed again.

A sound creaked into the stillness.

Whirling about, the elf saw the knob of the outside door turning gently. A head, topped with a tweed cap, came around the edge of the door as it slowly opened. A pair of blue eyes glanced about the room, coming to rest on the ancient sleeper by the fire. On the brown wrinkled face of the intruder, a crafty smile appeared. Stepping in softly, he closed the door behind him.

"A thief!" the elf shouted to himself.

"What's that? What's that?" stammered the plan, in great alarm.

"A thief! Thief! See him at the door! What will I do? What will I do?" The elf was running about in a frenzy, trying to think how he'd save this fine family from robbery. To be sure, their hospitality to the elf had been quite accidental and un-

aware, but he was sure they'd have been even politer if they'd known he was there, so he surely owed them his loyalty.

Suddenly he thought of his mischief trap.

Snatching his pocket-handkerchief bundle, he started fumbling to untie it.

"Your pocket, in your pocket!" shrieked the plan.

"What? Oh, yes, yes. Oh, my goodness. Oh, yes, here it is . . ." And flying into the path of the thief, he set his trap.

Down came the foot, snap went the trap, CRASH went the thief over a chair that had suddenly gotten in his way.

Granddad sprawled backwards in terror, yelling, "Ho, ho! Man the yardarms!"

Daisy rushed into the kitchen, her eyes staring. Behind her the children tumbled in excitement. "What's up?" they yelled. "Granddad, what's all the racket? What's it all about?"

But Granddad, leaning forward in his rocker, had recovered from his fright. Gazing intently at the chapfallen thief, who was busily righting the chair, he said slowly, "Mike McMahon, what do you think you're doin'?"

"Just—ah—trying to right this dratted chair, Steven," came the carefully casual reply. And Mr. McMahon, who apparently was not a thief after all, cocked his head and looked at Daisy and the children standing wild-eyed in the door. "Up kind of late, are you not?" he inquired of them.

Daisy lifted her eyebrows. "We *were*," she said pointedly, "we *were* in bed. Until people started making enough racket to rattle the saints."

Mr. McMahon sighed gustily. "Here I come," he said, "on a mission of cheer, to beguile the declining hours of my aged friend here, and what happens? I get a chair thrown at me, that's what happens!" Shaking his head, Mr. McMahon drew the chair in question close to the fire, and sat down.

"Threw a chair at you indeed," Daisy sniffed, but she was smiling now. "Why don't you look where you're going, Mike?"

"I was looking," Mike insisted, very puzzled. But he could see that no one quite believed him. He was beginning not to believe himself, since he knew that one second the chair hadn't been there, and the next he had tangled with it on the floor. "It's a queer one," he said, pulling perplexedly at his ear.

"Well, I'm off to bed again," said Daisy. "Come along, children. Dad, there's hot tea at the back of the stove for you and Mike." She went, herding the young ones before her.

The two old men sat regarding each other solemnly. Their mouths quivered with smiles. They grinned. They put back their heads and laughed loudly.

"Aged friend . . . declinin' hours . . . " laughed Granddad uproariously. "Mike, my lad, you gave me a turn for sure."

"No more than I gave myself, Steven."

[53]

"A fine thing, when a man can't get out of the way of a chair," chuckled Granddad.

Mike drew himself up firmly. "We'll have no more on the subject of that chair. It hurled itself at me. I prefer to forget it, since you . . ."

Suddenly Granddad leaned forward, struck with a new thought. "Mike," he said, looking furtively over his shoulder, "Mike, do you suppose . . ."

Head unmoving, Mike's eyes swept about the room. "You mean . . . the Little People?" he whispered hoarsely.

They stared at each other, and once again peered stealthily about. Granddad shook his shoulders. "Best not talk about it," he whispered back. Then, clearing his throat, he said loudly, "How about a spot of tea, Mike?" And they busied themselves with the hot brew.

"What Little People?" said a flutey voice behind them.

"Saints preserve us!" yelled Mike, spilling his tea on the stove and over his sweater.

"Emmett!" said Granddad breathlessly, "Emmett, don't be sneakin' up on people that way. It's enough to ice a man's heart over. Why aren't you in bed?"

The little boy regarded his great-grandfather serenely. "Not sleepy," he informed the two old men, who looked at each other helplessly. From Granddad's guilty appearance, it seemed that

Emmett was often entertained after the rest of the household had gone to bed.

"Emmett," he murmured coaxingly, "if I give you a mug of milk, will you run along to bed like the good boy?"

"Well," said Emmett, "if you tell me about the Little People, too, then I will." He tipped his head back and looked anxiously from one venerable face to the other.

All this time, the elf was listening in a daze. From disbelief, to astonishment, to joyous understanding that he had indeed found his Believer. Not only one, but two Believers. Trembling with excitement, he had watched his mischief trap do its work, and it was not until Mike had actually fallen to the floor with the chair that the elf realized what it meant.

Because of course if Mike hadn't believed in fairy people, he never would have been caught in the trap.

Thrusting the trap back into his pocket with shaking fingers, the elf kept his eyes on the two old men. Now, as Emmett questioned them, an expression of bewilderment flickered on the elf's tiny face. "Why two?" he said. "How is it that there are two?"

"Two Believers?" answered the plan, who was almost as happy as the elf. "That's easy. There's another elf somewhere."

"I never saw him. And I looked for years."

"You missed him, without a doubt. I have never known," the plan went on, "anyone who wanted to do and see everything

[55]

for himself the way you do. If all humans were like you, there wouldn't be a Believer anywhere. Can't you just know something without having to see it?"

Suddenly the elf saw that he was indeed a terrible doubter. The plan was right.

"And perhaps," the elf mused, "there are even more elves here and there in the world."

"I've thought so all along. But it's no use arguing with you, so I just said nothing. Anyway," the plan added, "I've enjoyed the trip."

"And so have I. You've been a good plan and a good friend," the elf said affectionately, apparently forgetting the times they'd disagreed.

The plan seemed content, too, remembering only the good times. He said, "I'm going to leave you now, Elf. We've done what we set out to do, and I must go on. But I won't forget you, and I'll speak of you from time to time in this head and that. Who knows, after a while the fairy troops may be back in the hills, the way they used to be . . . "

"Oh, Plan," called the elf, with a little sob, "good-bye. Oh, don't go . . . " But he could tell by a lightness in his head that the plan had already slipped away.

And now, he thought sadly, I'll have no one to think to. He felt immeasurably sad that just at his moment of triumph he should lose a friend.

It's strange, he went on in his thoughts, but now I realize what the frog meant when he said I couldn't do anything even if I did find my Believer. Because here he is, here two of him is, and I wouldn't be surprised if little Emmett becomes a third, and I can't do anything about it, except look at them and be grateful. I don't even want to. It's wonderful to know he's here—they're here—but now I think I'll go home.

Granddad was saying to Emmett, perched on his knees, "They aren't really bad little people, but they're devilish mischievous. And it doesn't do to talk about them too much, or go too near their fairy places . . . "

The elf smiled. Why, it's just like it used to be, he thought happily. He could hardly wait for Mike to leave, so the door would be opened and he could start back.

When he did, the sun was just coming up, like an orange meshed in the fog. But as he went away from the coast, in toward the hills, the air cleared. He went very fast, not stopping to visit, or eat, or sleep. So the return trip was much faster.

One morning when the world seemed as though it had been dipped in ice water and tossed in the sun to dry, the elf spied a little form hopping along the road in front of him. Very sadly it hopped. Hop, thud. Hop, thud.

Taking to his heels, the elf ran in pursuit, till he drew up beside the little hopper.

"Hello, Peeper," he said softly.

"Oh . . . *Elf*. Oh, hello!" cried the tiny frog joyfully. "I've been looking all over for you." He began to sob. "I thought you'd dissolved."

"Well, don't cry now," smiled the elf. "I'm back. And I think I'll be around now for a long time."

Together, they hurried back to the wild place.